FROM PRAGUE TO FLORIDA AND BACK

A DIARY OF DREAMS AND REALITY

I0553167

Lux Lucens

"This book isn't about perfection. It's about the courage to face the truth—and to return to yourself. Gently. With respect. And without shame."

— Lux Lucens

Illustrations by @Vallorea

This book is published by Prime Enterprises Media, 24. July 2025 by Amazon Kindle Direct Publishing printed over Amazon and independent platforms.

ISBN

978-80-11-06836-3 (e-Pub)

978-80-909-552-3-3 (Paperback)

978-80-11-06835-6 (PDF)

978-80-11-06837-0 (Mobi)

Dedication

This book is a work of fiction based on personal experiences and is intended for educational and awareness purposes only. The content explores themes related to family conflict and domestic violence in a general and human context. It does not represent or criticize any specific culture,

religion, government, or legal system. All characters and events are either fictional or used in a non-identifying manner. Any resemblance in this story to real persons, living or dead, location or events ispurely coincidental.

The author fully respects the laws, traditions, and values of The United Arab Emirates, USA and Czech Republic. The intent of this work is to support dialogue healing and understanding.

Contents

Introduction

This book was born out of silence. Out of the years of pretending everything was fine. That "it's not that bad." That if I just tried harder, understood more, forgave more, it would stop eventually.

It didn't.

I've been there. In the words that make you doubt yourself. In the looks that make you feel like you're losing your mind. In those moments when you smile on the outside while your voice is slowly dying on the inside. Writing this book was my way of reclaiming myself, piece by piece. And—just maybe—it can become your way too. Not because we share the same story, but because we know the same fear and hope.

I'm not a therapist. I'm simply a person who decided to speak to tell you this: You are not "too sensitive, weak or wrong." "You are perfect as you are — a unique soul. There is no one like you, and there never will be."

Maybe you're reading this book in secret. Maybe you're still in it. Maybe you've left, but inside, you still feel lost. Wherever you are, allow yourself to read slowly. Allow yourself to feel it. And allow yourself to believe that a world can exist for you too.

A world where there is peace. Where silence is not punishment. Where love doesn't hurt.

This is the beginning. The beginning of coming back to yourself.

From Prague to Florida

Jana was thirty, with five-month-old twin girls and a life that, from the outside, looked fine. But inside, she lived in constant tension. Her husband, Carl- Austrian by birth and a trained economist, was usually at work. When he did come home, it was late. He often passed out on the couch, reeking of alcohol.

The distance between them was growing. Whenever Jana tried to talk, Carl shut down or got defensive. Sometimes he wouldn't speak to her for days, punishing her with silence.

When she told him how hurt she felt when he broke promises or ruined their plans, he brushed her off with a smile. That smile made her feel small, foolish for opening up.

His message was clear: Don't bring it up again.

But problems don't disappear just because they're not discussed. They linger, unspoken. Carl's unresolved past, especially his strange emotional attachment to his ex, Agatha, crept between them like a shadow, dimming what light they had left. Agatha didn't want him back. She wanted him to suffer, just like he had made her suffer. Her messages were polite on the surface, but underneath was jealousy, bitterness, and a quiet hunger for revenge.

And he turned to secret drinking.

He never opened a bottle at home, never sat down with a glass of wine after a long day. His drinking happened in his car parked a few streets away. He'd return with sweat on his brow, a distant glaze in his eyes, and a breath Jana could identify before a single word was spoken. In the evening, he would vanish. And if he couldn't leave immediately, he found a reason to go such as a grocery run.

Jana began to see the pattern: tension came first, then the fight, then the door closing behind him.

But on weekends, everything felt almost normal. They spend the days outside, with the children, laughing, hugging and sharing simple moments. In the evenings, he grilled, experimented with marinades, watched the fire, and seemed happy. Those were the moments when he came alive again.

She used to tell him he could be a true "grill master," and he liked hearing that. Then one evening, he came to her and said he was selling the company.

"I have to, it would fail otherwise" he said quietly.

Jana didn't argue; she sensed the heaviness behind his words.

"Maybe," he added, "I could use the money to open a restaurant."

Jana had worked in restaurants herself — she knew how tough it could be.

"It might be enough to start with a small food stand," she gently suggested. But Carl dismissed her suggestion without a second thought.

"There are more opportunities in the United States right now, the U.S. is in the midst of an economic crisis." he insisted. Jana wasn't sure what she would do. Until now, Carl had been co-owner of a company managing

real estate for others. So she asked, "What exactly do you want to do?" But Carl had no real answer — only vague notions and scattered dreams.

Then, a few weeks later, Carl announced a new plan: they would move to the United States and open a German restaurant. For him, it was a fresh start — a way to escape what he refused to face in Prague.

To Jana, it sounded like another impulsive, grand idea. She said no. Carl ignored her answer.

The arguments grew. The exhaustion deepened. And eventually, Jana apologized and agreed to go. Not because she believed in his dream, but because she was too tired to keep fighting. She hoped that in a different country, she might find some peace. She imagined warmth, calm days, and space for her children to grow freely.

Carl flew to Florida first. He said he needed to prepare — find a restaurant space, arrange housing, hire lawyers, and start the visa process. He settled in Florida, in a rental apartment.

Not long after, Jana received a video from him. Carl looked relaxed, full of energy, and excited about the future.

He talked about a restaurant space— an old house that had been closed for years. He made it sound like things were finally falling into place.

Jana wanted to believe him. But a small part of her didn't. After months of conflict, emotional exhaustion, and feeling lost in her own marriage, she was drained. Two babies. So she gave in.

A few months later, she was on a plane with her niece and the little ones. Jana had promised her the usual nanny's wage and paid for all her expenses, so she could help with the children. The cabin was stifling and loud; the kids cried and screamed for the entire flight while fellow passengers glared in annoyance. Questions kept swirling in her mind. The beginning of a new life looked nothing like the dream she had imagined.

A New Beginning, Old Shadows

The apartment Carl rented was part of a low-rise complex lined with palm trees. There was a small pool, a playground, and everything looked clean, neat—almost idyllic. But inside, the apartment told a different story. The air was stale and heavy. Dust coated every surface.

The fridge reeked of mold. The washer was broken. The air conditioner wheezed and pushed out more dust than air. The place hadn't been cleaned. Not even the basics.

Jana tried calling the real estate agent. No help. "It's yours now," they said. "Ask the owner to fix it." The beds were broken. Splintered wood jutted out like old injuries. The nightstands wobbled. Nothing had been painted. No fresh start. Just the worn remains of someone else's neglect. Jana didn't cry. She rolled up her sleeves.

She called in a cleaning service to scrub the carpets, wash the sofa, and sanitize the beds. Every stain, every trace of dust felt like a ghost of the past being swept away. If this was her new life, it would not simply begin—it would be carved out, piece by piece, from the raw ground beneath her. Dust and all.

The restaurant Carl had leased was nearby. An older one-story building with a fading exterior, cracked parking lot, and a rusted sign frame from the business that came before. Inside, the AC rattled and an old refrigerator stood humming under a sign that read: "Do not unplug." But it was a place where someone could come, sit down, and eat. And for now, that was enough.

Carl managed the permits, renovations, and suppliers. He talked nonstop about the concept: authentic German food, no frills. Sausages. Schnitzels. Beer. The name he chose sounded like a joke. Jana didn't say anything. She had bigger concerns.

She was searching for both restaurant staff and a babysitter. She tried enrolling the children in various preschools, but each morning they cried when she dropped them off, and within a week,

they'd fall ill forcing her to keep them home once again. She cycled through three different preschools, one after another, but nothing worked. Eventually, she decided to look for a babysitter instead.

At first, she found an American babysitter. A young girl who had come to support Jana's niece. But Jana soon realized the babysitter was struggling too. So, she tried two more. One was a kind older lady who quickly grew tired, and the other seemed too strict with the children. Jana considered finding a babysitter through an agency, but the fees were too high. Then she posted on social media, and a Czech girl responded. She was currently in New York and was supposed to fly back to the Czech Republic but wanted to stay a bit longer. She offered to come right after Jana's niece.

At the same time, Jana was still searching for restaurant staff. It wasn't easy, but she eventually found a German cook. Alongside him came a woman who knew the local scene well and introduced Jana to servers and kitchen helpers she trusted. As the team slowly came together, Jana felt a glimmer of hope that the restaurant might succeed.

To her surprise, people showed up as soon as the restaurant opened. Locals, tourists, and expats—especially Germans in the area. They liked the food. Some became regulars. There was a buzz. Flags hung outside. Real German sausages from a local butcher. Homemade strudel, Schwarzwälder Kirsch Torte.

It looked like a success. In photos, they looked happy. At home, everything was falling apart. Carl drank more. By noon, he was already dulled. Cigarettes and vodka became his anchors.

At first, Jana tried to mirror him, hoping he might notice his own decline. She smoked, drank, and went to sleep. But he didn't care.

Another night, she drank until she passed out in front of the TV. He didn't react—if anything, he seemed more at ease.

A week later, she gently asked, "Are you okay? Can we talk?"

He admitted he had a problem. Promised to stop. But it was all for show—empty promises meant to quiet her, not change him.

He disappeared to the restaurant's back terrace each night, a cigarette in one hand, a glass in the other. The smoke curled into the darkness, drifting back through the open window.

Jana thought, *Maybe tonight he'll come back inside, sit with me, talk like he used to.* But all she heard was the scrape of his lighter, the clink of ice against glass, and the heavy silence that followed. *Is this what my life has become? Waiting for him to notice me? Hoping for scraps of attention while he drinks himself numb?* The thought burned more than the smell of smoke. She wanted to shake him, to drag him back to the man he once was. But instead, she lay still, knowing he was already slipping beyond her reach. Carl didn't talk to her anymore. He had someone else to talk to: Agatha.

When Jana pushed, he shrugged or walked away. He joked, dismissed her feelings. It felt like speaking to a wall—a wall that smoked and drank. She sat on the restaurant porch, listening to cicadas and the steady hum of the AC, wondering if this was freedom, or just another kind of trap. She knew now: Carl had a drinking problem. Alcohol dulled what he refused to face. He didn't want responsibility. He wanted to escape. Go back to being a carefree teenager, with no stress and no pressure.

Jana reached out to his family. She thought maybe they could convince him to get help. His sister Doreen responded politely but offered nothing useful. No advice. No support. Just: "Carl has always struggled with depression." That was it.

Jana saw it clearly: Doreen didn't want to help. Her own marriage was falling apart, and Carl's mess made hers feel smaller.

Carl's father tried. He begged. He shouted. Nothing worked.

Carl had already decided: he wasn't the problem. Jana was. She was too critical. Too demanding. Never satisfied. That's what he told himself. He didn't ask what he'd done wrong. He never questioned his role. He painted the future but delivered a nightmare.

A House Without Keys: Hope as a Trap

One morning, while Jana was home with the kids, the doorbell rang. Standing outside was the apartment's landlord. No call ahead. No apology. Just a flat statement that she had "forgotten something in the closet."

Without waiting for permission, she stepped inside. Said she was the owner. Walked straight to the bedroom. Opened a locked wardrobe. Took what she came for. Left. No thank-you. No explanation.

Jana stood frozen. A stranger had just walked through their private space, uninvited. This wasn't her home. It wasn't even her country. She had no keys, no voice, no safety.

That night ended in a fight.

Everything boiled over—the apartment, the money, the work, the kids. "I'm flying back to Prague," she said.

Carl stood up, fists clenched. "You're not going anywhere."

When she searched for flights, he ripped the laptop from her hands and locked her in the bedroom. "Buy it, and you'll see," he muttered.

Then, he raised his hand and hit her. Not hard. Not enough to bruise. But enough to send a message.

Jana froze. One question echoed: *Where is the line? And what happens when he crosses it?*

She sat in silence.

This wasn't about the fight or the alcohol. It was about power and control. And yet, part of her still clung to the belief that maybe, somewhere beneath the anger, he cared.

She didn't leave. She acted like nothing had happened.

Days later, another argument. This time at the restaurant. Carl sat at the desk, drinking. Jana stood, holding a folder, frustrated that he hadn't ordered supplies. The freezer was empty. She slammed the folder on the desk.

"You're acting like a general," he said.

"I'm not playing boss. I just want this place to run."

He leapt up, shouting. Then shoved her. She hit the wall. No injury. But clear intent.

He wasn't a partner anymore. He was an adversary. And somehow, she still blamed herself.

Now, she feared home and work. Then came silence. Days of it.

Until one evening, Carl walked in holding a real estate flyer.

"I found a house. Big yard. Let's start over." he said.

Four bedrooms. Close by. Beautiful, in the photo. And suddenly, she believed him again. She made herself believe.

Maybe this would change everything." If we have the house, he'll stop drinking. The kids will be happy. We'll make it," she told herself.

Soon after, a Czech au pair arrived from New York to help. She had come for a short stay but ended up staying a couple of months longer.

They checked out the house, and soon after, they booked it and signed the contract. Everything seemed to move quickly, but the day for the keys never came.

"The tenant hasn't moved out," said the notary. "Give it a week."

A week turned into a month. Still no keys. Savings dwindled. Carl kept drinking and making empty promises. Jana drove to the address. The tenant answered with a baby on his hip. "I haven't had time to move," he said. No apology. No deadline.

Jana decided to seek support through Legal Aid. A young attorney explained the steps. She drafted letters. Made calls. Followed up. They lived surrounded by boxes, by silence, by blame.

Each morning, Jana woke early. Made breakfast. Dressed the children. Answered questions she couldn't explain. Then left for work, keeping everything afloat. She did it all—payroll, orders, management—while Carl kept receipts and typed a few numbers into a spreadsheet. And watched her, quietly jealous.

Two months passed. Then, one afternoon, an SMS: *"The house is empty. Keys are in the mailbox."*

No explanation. She drove to pick up the keys with Carl. They opened the door. The space was dusty. Quiet. But it was finally theirs—at least on paper.

Carl smiled beside her, as if he'd made it all happen. As if he'd forgotten who had done all the work.

The moving began—repairs, cleaning, painting, the garden, organizing. Exhausting. But she could breathe again. Not with happiness, but with preparation. She held the keys in her hand—not just to the house, but to her next decision.

The Court

They thought it was all finally behind them. They told the apartment owners they were moving into their own place but got no reaction. So, they moved out and left the keys with the agent.

A new house. A fresh beginning.

Then came the lawsuit.

The landlords of the apartment Jana and Carl had rented filed a case. They claimed the couple had overstayed illegally and owed money for both unpaid rent and damage to furniture. Jana had tried reaching the landlord to ask what she owed for the extra two weeks. Her calls were ignored. The new house hadn't even been handed over yet. They had no choice but to stay put. Still, the landlord demanded thousands for "lost rent" and "damaged furnishings." Never mind that the fridge had mold, the furniture was already broken, and the apartment hadn't been cleaned when they moved in.

Jana read the summons, heart sinking. They were being sued. The courtroom was cold, impersonal. The mediator tried to ease the tension. The landlord, confident, demanded over $10,000. Jana clutched her folder of documents: proof of payments, messages about repairs, photos. But the judge barely looked up, uninterested. The landlord showed photos of the apartment's condition and claimed damage to items that were already broken.

Carl stayed silent. Jana wasn't allowed to explain. She was only asked if she accepted fault. She tried, but her English faltered.

The judge grew impatient. At the end, he acknowledged one receipt: Jana had paid for professional cleaning. He deducted $150 from the total. She tried again to present her evidence. The judge cut her off. "Give it to the court officers," he said. He didn't want to hear more. The verdict: pay $10,000. Jana sat frozen. She had come to America to build a life, not to lie or cause trouble. But the system had branded her otherwise. On the way home, Carl muttered something about lawyers and injustice. He said it was "temporary." But something inside Jana cracked. And something inside her no longer trusted him. That evening, he poured her a glass of wine and said: "We'll get through this. Everything will be okay. Just hold on a bit longer."

"But those words no longer worked. He used them every time things fell apart. Every time she needed answers, he gave her promises. "I've almost got it sorted." Nothing ever got sorted.

Jana began to see clearly: Carl never intended to fix anything. He just postponed. If she asked questions, his tone shifted: "You're always stressing me out." or "Do you know how hard this is for me?"

Everything she said came back as blame. As if she was the problem. The one ruining everything.

In the evenings, Carl drank more. At first it was glasses of wine. Then straight from the bottle. Sometimes he disappeared without a word. Sometimes he came back restless— too sweet or ice cold. He spoke about Agatha. Said she still wrote him.

Another betrayal. Carl gave Agatha his apartment. Claimed it was out of friendship. But Agatha didn't forgive him for marrying Jana. She wanted revenge. Her advice was toxic, her presence constant. She encouraged Carl to fight Jana, not love her. Jana later found Agatha's online posts.

She belonged to a spiritual group in Prague that performed dark rituals. It gave Jana chills.

Carl once asked if he could send Agatha pictures of their children. Jana said no. He sent them anyway.

When Jana found out, Carl downplayed it: *"It's not that serious."* But it was. Jana couldn't build a life with a man still clinging to another woman's attention.

A real relationship needs respect, boundaries, and honesty— especially when things get hard. And the more contact Carl had with Agatha, the more the kids cried at night, restless, unable to sleep.

Jana couldn't shake the feeling that something unseen was affecting them. Jana worked. She managed the business. She raised the kids. She handled legal issues, bills, broken appliances. And still, Carl made her feel like she was failing. She started writing down the things he said:

"You're the strong one, so you handle it."

At the Restaurant

An open beer at the bar. A glass of wine "for tasting" in the kitchen. At first, Jana saw it only at the edges. She figured a little drinking might be normal in the restaurant world and didn't want to micromanage. But then the chef moved slower at night.

The waitress was louder, laughing too much, drinking with a customer after lunch hours.

One evening, while doing inventory, Jana heard laughter coming from the kitchen.

She opened the door and saw her husband, drink in hand, toasting with two employees. A bottle of vodka sat open on the table, next to a half-eaten plate of sausages.

"Is this normal?" she asked, her voice low but sharp

"Jana, relax," her husband replied, smiling in a way that felt hollow. "Everyone's worked hard. Let them enjoy a little break."

But it didn't feel like a break to her. Every ignored rule, every excuse, every joke made at her expense chipped away at her authority. She tried to enforce order, but it was no use. The staff saw her as a formality. If they waited, they could get a different answer from him. One with fewer rules. They began sidestepping her. Quietly, but obviously. Beer boots went missing. Vodka bottles turned up in the freezer. The kitchen echoed with laughter too casual for a busy shift.

When Jana raised concerns, her husband dismissed them. "It's our culture," he said. "Letting loose helps them stay loyal." But it wasn't one shot. And it wasn't after hours.

Employees ignored her corrections. If a guest complained, she couldn't act on it without her husband's sign-off. The same husband who now held court at the bar every night, drinking with regulars, lost in a fog she remembered from Prague.

One day, she brought up a missed meat order and the mess in the kitchen. She overheard the chef, Max, mutter to a line cook, "Don't worry, she's just the wife. He's the boss. She should stay home." Her stomach turned. Her husband said nothing. He was helping build a business where she no longer had a voice. That night, she tried to talk to him again. The kids were asleep. He sat on the couch with a wine bottle, eyes locked on the TV.

"This can't go on," she said.

"What now?" he sighed.

"The staff doesn't listen. This isn't a bar. It's not a college party."

"You don't get it," he said. "This isn't Czechia. It works differently here."

After that, it got worse. Her ideas were ignored. The staff treated her like a nuisance.

Domestic Violence

It was an evening like many before. The children were asleep. Jana came home from the restaurant, exhausted, wearing silence in place of words. She dropped her keys on the table and slipped off her shoes.

Her husband was outside at the table. An open bottle of wine sat beside him. His eyes were cloudy but alert. He was waiting.

"You were there that long again? You know how I feel when you're always gone."

Jana answered evenly. She told him she'd been working, that she was doing the best she could. No blame, just fact. That was enough.

He stood abruptly, knocking over the chair. He shouted. Accusations, disconnected, irrational, tumbled out. How she left him alone. How she embarrassed him. How she didn't trust him. Then came the profanity. She said nothing. And her silence made him angrier.

She turned away. That's when it happened. He pulled her back, strong hands around her neck. Not tight enough to bruise. But enough to choke off breath. Enough to stun her still. Enough to paralyze the air in her lungs.

"You never listen to me," he growled. "You think you're better? That you can handle everything and I'm weak?" She couldn't speak. But inside, her thoughts were clear: He is the weak one. And he knows it. That's why he drinks. Drinking let him escape, not from her, but from himself.

He let go. Sat back down. Lit a cigarette. Said nothing. And she just stood there. Shaking. But she didn't cry. Not anymore. The night sank into silence. Jana stood alone in it, knowing now that another line had been crossed. And that no house, no place, could fix this.

Cracks

Jana still hoped something would change — maybe in him, maybe in her — and they'd return to the path they once, even from a distance, called shared. But slowly, day by day, she saw every hopeful word dissolve into silence.

Maybe there was still a chance. Maybe his father would talk to him. He did. Nothing changed.

The atmosphere had been heavy for a long time. But now, Carl spoke to her differently, sharper, meaner. That humiliating tone he once saved for arguments became his normal voice. Or worse, he said nothing at all. Sometimes for days. Just to win.

He showed up when she didn't ask. Stayed silent when she tried to talk about the kids. Dismissed her when she offered to help with accounting. Ignored her when she mentioned the thefts in storage.

"Silence, Jana. Shut up, you bitch. All you do is complain," he said one evening between swigs of vodka. He wasn't drunk. Just cold. Calculated. Loud. Angry. When they got home, he screamed, waking the children on purpose. To feel power. To show it. That night, he slapped her. Hard. In front of the children. Their cries filled the room. He made sure they saw. And then, as if it meant nothing, he took the keys and left.

The next morning, police found him asleep in the car. Empty vodka bottle beside him. On the phone screen, a message to his ex-girlfriend. He'd called Jana "a burden." The police arrested him. That morning, her phone rang. His lawyer. Her hands shook — not from fear, but from exhaustion. Quiet, deep, worn-out. He was in jail. The bond had to be paid. She said yes. And Carl came back. But with him came the fear of what would happen next.

That evening, after the kids had fallen asleep, Jana opened her laptop. She searched for a divorce lawyer who helped foreigners. A woman named Clara came up. Her website had a calm smile and a line that caught Jana's eye: "I help women find their voice again." Jana wrote a short email. No details. No emotion. Just facts: Two kids. Austrian husband. Domestic abuse, mostly emotional, with one recent physical assault. Shared business, but he had full control. She sent it. Her hands stopped shaking an hour later. And in that quiet, she realized something had shifted. Maybe she was starting to find her voice again. With a deep breath, she clicked Send.

At the Breaking Point

The lawyer responded the next day. Brief. Professional. But with a warmth that brought tears to Jana's eyes. "We'll arrange a personal meeting. I'll explain your rights and how to protect yourself and your children. You are not alone in this." That day, she didn't speak to Carl. That night, she slept in a different room — on the

couch, phone under her pillow.

She was ready to run or call for help. She felt like a stranger in her own life. When she woke with her heart pounding at a shadow that wasn't real, she stayed awake. She couldn't risk falling asleep again.

His words still rang in her head: "Bitch, I'll destroy you. Everything you have is mine."

And yet she had sold the property in Prague, cancelled her savings, and sent all the

money into their joint account. Every bill was paid from that account. She had nothing left that was just hers.

The next few days passed in a blur. At the restaurant, she worked, but everyone sensed something was off. Carl was drunk at work when she arrived. Another night, he didn't show up at all.

She found him at midnight asleep in the car. Engine running, German pop music still playing. She left him there. By morning, a neighbour rang the doorbell. "Get him out of the car or someone's calling the police."

It was too late.

Before she could think, police, ambulance, and firefighters arrived. They pulled Carl out of the car and onto the ground. Jana stood at the door, children in her arms, watching.

He wasn't injured. Just hungover.

They left. He went to bed and slept the day away.

The next morning, he waited for her in the kitchen. Sober, but with that cold, bitter look the kind you get after too many lonely nights with your own silence. "You called the police on me? You want to destroy me? What kind of mother are you? You'd be nothing without me. Nowhere!"

She didn't answer. That only fuelled him.

He accused her of flirting with the chef. Claimed she planned to steal the restaurant. Said she wanted to get rid of him so she could "show off" with the lawyer. He shouted so loudly the children hid in the bathroom.

Then came the blow, fast, open-handed, across her face. Pain sharp and blunt.

Something cracked in her. Not from fear. From clarity.27 She ran outside and called the police.

When they arrived, Carl stood on the stairs, waving a small pair of scissors,

threatening to kill himself if they arrested him again. Officers drew their guns. In the

end, he surrendered.

They took him to jail.

But this time, the kids had seen it. The police documented it. And Jana had a lawyer. That night, she sat at the kitchen table, head in her hands. She didn't cry. She just listened to the quiet. For the first time in years, it wasn't frightening. It was hers.

The Boss Sleeps on the Table

The protection order was issued quickly. Lawyer Clara was efficient, precise, and unyielding, exactly what Jana needed. The temporary order prohibited Carl from approaching the children or the house. On paper, she had peace. But reality played by different rules.

Money was draining fast, legal fees, visa renewal, bond payments, Carl's new lease. On the other side stood his lawyer, a bitter man in a suit who hated his wife and carried that same contempt toward Jana. He never said it directly, but his demeanour made it clear: he saw her as the villain ruining a business.

In the meeting with Clara, he wore a smug smile, repeating "alleged violence" as if it were all just a misunderstanding.

Jana shivered. Clara stayed composed, her steady presence Jana's only anchor in the storm.

Meanwhile, the restaurant was unravelling. A business without clear leadership, or worse, one under a drunk's command, was bound to sink.

Max, the chef Carl once praised, turned out to be just like him. Talented, yes. But lost to alcohol. He drank before and during shifts. Food came out cold, meat undercooked, sauces off.

Guests started to complain. At first, the reviews were mild. Then came harsher words: disappointment, not authentic, drunk owner unpleasant.

The protection order kept Carl from the house, but not the restaurant. He began showing up again. Jana and Carl had to coordinate shifts, but he came anyway — just to eat, drink, and ruin things. He'd stagger in drunk, order beer and sausage, then pass out at a table. Sometimes he woke up, yelled for more wine, and scared the last customers away.

Other times, he berated the staff in front of diners. Once, he knocked over a tray of glasses and walked off laughing. Another time, he vomited near a table, unfazed by the disgusted faces. When Jana wasn't there, he took cash from the register, invited his buddies in for free drinks, left lights on overnight, and scattered joints and cigarette butts behind the bar. Staff began to quit.

Some gave no notice. Others left with quiet apologies. "It's not working," one waiter told her. Jana felt the business slipping through her fingers. Like sand, no matter how tightly she tried to hold on. Daily sales dropped. A month after Carl's arrest, the restaurant was half-empty.

She started to wonder, was there anything left worth saving? Only five employees remained, and they gave her just enough courage to keep going.

But one night, she sat alone in the restaurant. The lights were off, except for a dull bulb above the bar. The ticking clock echoed through the quiet, louder than it should have. Time was marching on. The air felt heavy. Frustration hung in it. So did helplessness. Everything was failing: the stove blinked a warning, the A/C was dying, the extractor hoods needed cleaning, pest control was overdue, laundry bills were pending, the freezer was failing. Every fix needed money.

Her head filled with tasks, the list kept growing. And even though she could feel it ending, she stayed. Sat in that air, in that silence. It wasn't just the end of a business. Or a marriage. It was the end of who she used to be. Everything she tried had brought her here, to this dark, broken place. The restaurant. The dream. All of it in ruins. Sales kept falling. The room kept emptying. And Jana finally asked herself if saving anything still made sense.

Fear and Debts

Accounting had never been Jana's passion, but now it was the only thing she could control. She sat at the kitchen table, surrounded by unopened envelopes and threatening emails about late payments. The more numbers she stared at, the clearer it became how dire the state of the business really was.

Three months of unpaid rent. Refrigerator repair, denied, because the technician had never been paid last time. Air conditioning, one unit buzzed, another cooled unevenly, and the third was broken. The kitchen felt like an oven.

Guests complained and then disappeared. And her husband? Instead of fixing anything, he sent bonuses to those who stayed loyal, meaning the ones who didn't ask questions and drank or smoked with him after their shifts.

The biggest expense was Chef Max's salary. Jana couldn't believe her eyes. The bonus alone could've paid five full-time staff in Florida. And yet: the refrigerator was broken, food undercooked, and Max was bringing his own alcohol to work, hiding it in the storage room.

The restaurant's reputation was fading. The guests who remained were either clueless tourists or regulars who came just to sit and talk. That evening, when the refrigerator finally stopped working, Jana decided.

She walked into the kitchen where Max leaned against the sink, talking on the phone. He didn't even look at her.

"Max," she said calmly. "Huh?" "You're done. Today's your last day."

At first, he laughed. He thought she was joking. When he realized she wasn't, he started yelling. Then he called Carl.

Carl showed up thirty minutes later, face red with alcohol and rage.

"You have no right! Max stays! The chef is essential!" Carl shouted.

"Essential for what? An empty business and spoiled food?" Jana replied.

"You're embarrassing me!" Carl shouted.

"You've turned embarrassment into a daily routine." Jana said.

For the first time, she looked at him without fear. Just tired. Just done. He stood against her, but he wasn't stronger. Just louder. Max left. And with him, a few loyal regulars. But Jana knew: if the restaurant had any chance, a cut had to be made. She turned to the only people she could trust. Her parents. Her father tried to calm her down, promising he would protect them no matter what. But still, every time Jana saw a strange car circling the house, or when someone mysteriously broke the water pipe in the garden, Jana froze.

Gertrude

Gertrude was a woman with a talent you couldn't ignore. Her homemade spätzle were excellent, soft, rich, the kind you remember from childhood visits to your grandmother.

When she joined the restaurant, she quickly won over guests and gradually gained the trust of her colleagues.

She acted like a friend, often saying, "You and I, we've got each other's backs, right Jana?" And Jana, though naturally cautious, eventually let her guard down.

When she started to work for Jana, she showed up with what seemed like a generous gift.

"I have this old German wood and glass cabinet. It doesn't fit in my place anymore, I want you to have it. It would look perfect in your restaurant." she spoke.

Jana was touched. She found a spot for it, carefully arranged her glasses inside. It became part of her restaurant.

But now, without warning, the cabinet was gone. No message. No explanation. One afternoon, when Jana was not at work,

Gertrude came by, took the cabinet back, and disappeared. She never came to the restaurant again. No resignation. No goodbye. Word got out: she had quickly opened her own place, a new restaurant, with the head chef Max. She had taken not just the cabinet, but the friendship and Jana's trust.

Jana was left without the cabinet. Without a second cook. Without a friend. But, also, without illusions, that people always mean what they offer. Sometimes, they give you something beautiful—

only to take it back when you're not looking. Gertrude did that. And once it happened, Jana learned to protect her heart and to choose people based on her intuition, not just their words.

Shortened Hours

In the restaurant, it felt as if someone had turned off the tap, leaving just enough to keep things from drying up completely. After the Czech babysitter left, Jana quickly realized that finding a reliable replacement wasn't just hard—it had to be affordable. She didn't have the money to hire another a full-time employee, and she needed to be at the restaurant herself.

One babysitter seemed perfect—young, enthusiastic, and willing to work for less. But it didn't take long before she became unavailable, saying she was moving away.

Another babysitter was sprinting after the girls through the neighborhood like a frantic soccer mom in overtime before she finally gave up. Meanwhile, a neighbor called Jana to say her daughters were running around outside all by themselves. In reality, the kids were teasing the babysitter and running away from her because she was strict, and they wanted to be mischievous.

Next was someone with her own little hurricanes at home—three kids running their own circus. Jana's daughters came back with stories of "mean looks" and "strict rules" that made them feel more like prisoners than guests. Jana wasn't sure if she was hiring a babysitter or a warden.

Then came the lady with three kids of her own who seemed to forget she was watching Jana's girls too. Between juggling her own chaos and Jana's kids, the babysitter was stretched so thin that the girls started calling her "The Invisible Woman." Jana worried constantly, wishing she could be in two places at once.

There was another babysitter who was nice and had a daughter the same age as Jana's girls, which seemed promising at first. But week by week, she kept asking for more money, making it harder for Jana to keep up.

The last one was sweet but... let's just say "unprepared and messy" is putting it mildly. On a day trip with the kids, she ran out of gas and improvised a heroic journey: walking the kids to the nearest gas station carrying a jerry can, like a scene from a low-budget family adventure movie. Another time, Jana decided to drop by her house unexpectedly. What she found looked less like a home and more like a laundry tornado had hit.

There were piles of dirty clothes spilling out of baskets, strewn across the floor like abandoned soldiers. Dishes sat forgotten in the sink, some still crusted with food from who-knows-when.

Dust bunnies had gathered in the corners like they were throwing a party. Jana's eyes widened in horror, and she took a cautious step back. It wasn't just clutter—it was a full-blown hygiene nightmare.

Jana tried to keep a polite smile, but inside she was thinking, *How on earth am I supposed to trust someone like this with my kids?* The thought of little hands grabbing toys from under mountains of mess gave her chills.

Despite the chaos, the babysitter was warm and caring. But for Jana, the idea of a clean, safe environment for her daughters was non-negotiable. After that visit, she realized that good intentions weren't quite enough—especially when paired with this level of mess.

Babysitter roulette was exhausting. Jana was juggling shifts at the restaurant and the constant anxiety over who was watching her children. It was funny, it was tragic, and it was real. But despite it all, she kept spinning the wheel—because what choice did she have?

Her kids would quickly get restless, so she couldn't keep them with her late into the night. Still, sometimes she brought them along to the restaurant, where they helped by cutting vegetables and running small errands. Together, they found little moments of fun amidst the busy work. In the restaurant, it started to feel like someone had turned off the tap, leaving just enough to keep things from drying up completely.

Jana closed the restaurant for lunch. The kitchen now opened only at five in the afternoon. She had fewer employees, fewer chances for revenue, but also less chaos. She had learned to manage the operation on her own. She often stood at the stove, served food, took orders. She was functioning. But at what cost?

She came home exhausted. The children knew she would arrive and be quiet. Maybe she'd tell a story. Then fall asleep standing up. One evening, when she came home after closing, her husband was waiting in the doorway.

He had no business being there, the restraining order made that clear. He shouldn't be there, but he came and he was drunk again. He spoke quietly, in a slick, slow voice, like someone who knew he had nothing left to lose.

When she told him to leave, he grabbed her by the arm. First gently, then harder. And when she managed to pull free, he grabbed her by the throat. He threw her to the ground. And kicked her. Once. Then he hit her, again and again, with his fists. It lasted only seconds, but for the first time, Jana felt he could truly hurt her. That it wasn't just a threat. It was real. Her heart raced, but her legs didn't fail her. She ran out of the house and called the police and they arrested him.

The exhaustion was deep. Physical, yes, but mostly mental. Everything looked almost right, but nothing felt easy. Then she noticed: Carl had taken her gold jewelry.

Jana finally saw it clearly. She had been in a toxic relationship.

A victim of domestic violence. She had read about this kind of thing before, and now she understood the patterns. There were no rules. Only unpredictable extremes. Sometimes things seemed good.

But just as quickly, they turned bad, leaving her unsure of where she stood. The constant stress of not knowing what would happen next had stolen her peace. Now, with clarity, she saw it all differently. The bad far outweighed the good.

A few days later, he posted bail, sold his car, and with that money, flew to Germany. She had been trapped in a cycle: broken promises, excuses, fights, neglect, disrespect, emotional abuse, physical pain, lies, manipulation, and then back to empty promises again. The realization hit like fresh air. Painful, but necessary. The pattern had been there all along. And for too long, she had been caught in a grip she hadn't understood before.

No Way Back

The days dragged on like a heavy thread that refused to break. Jana spent most of her time in the restaurant's office, where there was no longer a clear line between day and night.

Papers, invoices, phone calls with suppliers, nothing was improving. She couldn't shake the feeling that her world was slowly, but surely, collapsing.

And then came a new problem. One she hadn't expected. While reviewing the lease agreement, she discovered it was binding for several years. But Jana didn't have the money for rent.

She tried to explain the situation to the property manager, hoping he would plead her case to the landlord, or allow her to exit early.

He didn't seem sympathetic.

A few days later, the phone rang. It was the property manager. "Good afternoon, Jana. I wanted to let you know I've spoken with the owner. You'll remain in the lease. There's no option for early termination. The contract is binding. If you walk away, you'll be facing hundreds of thousands in penalties, and you'll most likely lose your personal property."

Jana froze. She had agreed to the lease terms back when she still had hope, hope that the business and her family would succeed. But she hadn't known all the details.

Carl had. Or maybe even he hadn't. And now, with everything at rock bottom, there was no money left to buy her freedom.

"But I don't have the money for rent…" she whispered.

"That's not our concern, Jana. The rent is due. We're open to discussion if you can present a plan to keep the lease going. If not, we'll proceed legally."

His voice was cold. So simple. As if he had never faced financial hardship, a failing business, or an abandoned marriage.

For a moment, Jana felt like she might break. One more call like this could've shattered her. But not this time. She didn't hang up like before. This time, she did something her husband never could: she stood on her own two feet. After a long pause, no longer afraid of the consequences, she made a decision and replied, "If I don't find a solution, I'll have no choice but to leave."

She didn't beg anymore. She hung up the phone, closing that chapter firmly behind her.

Second Chance, Same Ending

The ad to sell the restaurant had been online for several weeks. No big expectations, no aggressive marketing, just a quiet SOS Jana sent into the world.

This time, without illusions. It wasn't about ambition. It wasn't about saving anything. It was about ending it, she

needed to close what had long since fallen apart.

To everyone's surprise, someone responded.

A younger man, German, an entrepreneur who wanted to open a new concept in Florida: fast European food with restaurant-quality meals at bistro prices. He liked the location, the equipment,

and the fact that the restaurant already had permits and infrastructure. He offered a fair price.

It wasn't a miracle, but it was enough for Jana to pay off her debts and finally start something new. Even more, Jana had already made a deal with Carl that they would go into it together.

He said he wanted to "finally do something right."

But he had one condition: Jana wouldn't show up in court for the domestic violence case. His lawyer manipulated her so thoroughly that Jana began to feel like she would be the bad one if she didn't agree.

Carl also claimed he wanted everything to end with dignity. There was no conflict.

They spoke calmly, constructively. She believed them. For a moment, it seemed like they were finally closing this wrecked chapter.

The broker prepared the contract.

The signing of the sale was scheduled for Monday at 10:00 a.m. Jana got up early, sent the children to daycare, wore a simple black dress, her hair tied in a neat bun.

Jana felt hopeful. She sat in the broker's office; the buyer had already arrived, and the broker was ready.

But her husband didn't show up. No message. No call.

As if the moment had been completely erased from the calendar.

At first, the buyer was patient, but time kept ticking. Finally, he closed his folder and said: "I'm sorry, Jana. Your husband is not serious. Your business deserves a second chance, but I have my doubts. It's been closed several times before official hours.

I'm not about to chase your husband or customers. I can't afford to waste more time."

And he left.

Jana remained seated. Slowly, she stood, grabbed her jacket, walked out of the office, and didn't look back.

The Body Said Enough

All that remained was hunger. Not the symbolic kind, the real one.

One day, Jana stood in front of an empty fridge in her own kitchen and realized she didn't even have enough for basic groceries. Not for herself, not for the children. It wasn't any better at the restaurant, there was no money to buy ingredients.

To make things worse, her husband had unplugged the fridge and freezer, so everything spoiled.

There was no flour, no meat, no oil. Empty mustard jars stared back at her. Supplies were disappearing faster than hope. She didn't even have the strength to look at the bills anymore. At one point, she sat down on the cold kitchen floor and quietly admitted to herself: I need cash. Now. Right now. For food.

First, Jana asked her mother back in the Czech Republic to sell some of the things she had stored at her house—golf equipment, furniture, clothes, and even her gold jewellery. It wasn't about sentiment anymore. What she once treasured or saved for "someday" now had to help her get through today.

Her mother sounded surprised when they spoke on the phone.

"Are you sure?" she asked gently as Jana listed off the items.

Yes," Jana said without hesitation. I can't do this any other way."

She hoped the sales would bring in at least something. Not a fortune, just enough to cover another month. Things had lost their meaning now, but her gold jewellery was the hardest to part with. Some of it had been gifted to her; some she had bought while traveling—small treasures wrapped in big memories of family, love, and adventure. But even those had to go.

Her mother did what she could. She sent Jana some money right away—the full amount she had available in her own account, knowing Jana needed immediate help even if she hadn't asked outright.

"It's not much," she texted, "but I hope it helps. "Jana was deeply grateful. She knew this wouldn't save her, but she had learned to live in short bursts—taking life day by day, not weeks ahead. Just get through today, and maybe tomorrow. That same evening, she sent out several résumés.

The next morning, she put on an orange tank top and black shorts with the Hooters logo. She didn't think about what others might say. In the mornings, she worked as a waitress, forcing a smile, clenching her teeth when someone touched her back or made a crude joke.

In the afternoons, she rushed to her own restaurant, bringing whatever ingredients she could manage so the one cook could prepare food. She opened only for dinner — four hours, just long enough to earn enough to buy a few ingredients for the next day. She ran the bar herself, with one cook in the kitchen.

And in the evenings? She started another shift. At one of the more upscale restaurants

on the coast. She waited tables there too. Whatever she earned in tips went straight to groceries and childcare.

Three jobs. Three different worlds. One body. And no time. She couldn't be with them, but she could feed them. And for now, that was everything.

But very soon, her body began to scream. It started as a faint discomfort—a dull throb deep in Jana's jaw.

At first, she barely noticed it. Just a mild annoyance that came and went. But the ache soon grew sharper, pulsing with every bite and every sip of something hot or cold. The pain became relentless, creeping into her thoughts and stealing her focus

Jana tried to ignore it, pushing through the days with the same determination she always had. But the tooth pain was stubborn, a constant reminder that something was wrong.

Each morning, she woke with a slight pressure. Each night, it kept her awake just a little longer. She knew she couldn't put it off much more. The pain was no longer just physical; it weighed on her spirit, adding to the heavy days she was already carrying.

After two weeks, she decided to see a German dentist, trusting he would be more precise and reliable.

He examined her and told her she needed a crown. There was a serious infection, and he would have to clean the entire area thoroughly. The crown would cost several thousand dollars, but he offered a payment plan. Jana didn't hesitate—she went ahead with the procedure. When the crown was finally in place, she felt discomfort for a few more weeks, as if something still

wasn't quite right. But eventually, she got used to it. It was still better than the pain she'd been living with before.

Meanwhile, her mother made calls, met with buyers, and negotiated prices. After a few weeks, she managed to transfer more money from the sales. Each item sold felt like shedding a layer of Jana's former life. And maybe, in that letting go, there was a kind of freedom. The less Jana carried, the more space she had for something new. With the money she received, Jana paid off some credit card debt, freeing up funds she might need later.

One late night, everything seemed normal. Jana got home from her third shift around midnight, lay down for a few hours, and when she woke, her body felt unbearably heavy, like someone had poured sand into her bloodstream. Her kidneys ached, as if someone were digging their nails into her from behind, right under her ribs. But she said nothing. Her head was spinning. Her body didn't whisper. It screamed.

Still, she got up and made breakfast for the kids. Then she went to buy medicine. But just a few steps from the pharmacy, her knees gave out. A sharp pain struck her, and everything went dark. The last thing she remembered was the cold pavement against her cheek, and someone shouting as they ran toward her.

She woke in a hospital bed. She lay still, the IV steadily feeding into her bloodstream. Monitors surrounded her. A doctor stood nearby, calm but firm, telling her that her body couldn't go on any longer. Kidney infection. Severe exhaustion. Dehydration.

"You have to stop working, or whatever you're doing, immediately," the doctor told her.

"Your body just gave you its final warning."

Jana only nodded. Quietly. She didn't have the strength to argue. Or cry.

The news reached her husband.

They called him from the hospital. He came. For the first time in a long time, he wasn't

arrogant. He didn't blame her. He didn't insult her. He said nothing. He only asked Jana

if he could bring her home.

She agreed. She didn't have the power to resist.

When he brought Jana to the bedroom, he left. Jana overheard him calling his father in Germany.

"I really need your help. Jana was in the hospital. We can't pay the rent."

His father, a stern man who had never formed a warm relationship with Jana but had

always cared for the children, was surprised. But in the end, he sent them money he had

saved. Not much, but enough. Enough to cover the basics. Food. Rent. Medicine.

At home, Jana sat in silence. For the first time in weeks, she didn't have to do anything.

And in that stillness, in the pain and exhaustion, she began to feel something new: not anger, not frustration, but a pure and deep fatigue.

She finally knew: she couldn't live like this anymore.

An Offer That Doesn't Feel Like Another Trap

When Jana returned to the restaurant, the restaurant was silent. The freezer was broken,

and the tables were covered in a thin layer of dust. A grocery list hung in the kitchen, ingredients she couldn't afford. Jana stood there like a stranger in her own business.

This time, she knew it couldn't be saved. Not at this cost.

She had nothing left to sacrifice. She made her decision, calmly, without tears. She was ready to let it go. To close the restaurant. That same day, she sat down in the restaurant's office and started writing emails: a

closure notice, a list of equipment for sale, thank-you notes to suppliers and the last loyal customers. It felt almost like writing an obituary. And that's when he reached out.

He always sat at the table in the corner, she remembered. A friend of the chef, Max, he liked to eat Weisswurst or schnitzel with potato salad. He didn't talk much, but he always smiled. Now he came in person. He brought a flower and a business card. "I heard you're closing," he said. "That would be a shame."

Jana gave a tired smile. "I can't do it anymore. I'm not a banker or a superhero. The restaurant needs capital, repairs, management. And I... I'm done."

The man nodded gently. "I understand. That's why I want to offer you a solution. I'll buy the restaurant business. For a fair price. I'm not trying to get rich. I just like this place, and I believe it could come back to life. And you, if you want, you can stay. Help out. Work here. Or not. It's up to you. No obligations. Just a possibility. The only thing I ask is that you don't open another German restaurant within 70 miles."

An offer that didn't feel like another trap.

Jana just stared at him in silence for a moment. In her mind flashed every failure, every disappointment, every man who had made promises and then disappeared. But this man just looked at her. Quietly. Without expectations. Without pressure. For the first time in a long time, she felt something wasn't being forced, but offered. A door, simply… open.

Not a New Beginning

Jana accepted the offer without euphoria, but with calm, like finally settling down

a heavy suitcase you've been dragging for years.

The new owner, Mr. Schneider, hired an auditor, brought in a lawyer, and got to work. He didn't act like a savior, he acted like a professional. He knew what he was doing. And he had one condition: everything had to be transparent.

"You'll receive the agreed amount," he said quietly. "But it will go directly toward

the debts. I'll pay the creditors myself, not because I don't trust you, but because I want this to stay clean."

Jana nodded. She didn't care anymore. All she wanted was peace. No lawsuits. No collection threats. No more shame.

Mr. Schneider paid the overdue rent, the unpaid invoices for food supplies, and the

remaining wages for the staff. Together, they visited the accounting firm that had refused to release Jana's records, partly due to Carl's debts, partly due to Carl himself. The firm had no empathy for her position. Mr.

Schneider paid off part of the debt just to retrieve the basic paperwork. The results weren't great.

The company was deep in debt. So, he decided to purchase only the restaurant and its equipment, but not the troubled legal entity.

Her husband got his cut. He demanded it through his lawyer in a formal letter. He took the money. He didn't send a thank-you. Not even a message. Just a receipt. And silence.

Jana didn't mind. She paid what she could. Hired a new accountant. Followed his advice. For now, she stayed on as a shift manager, not as the owner. And she knew: once the company was gone, her work permit would follow. But she no longer tried to save anything. She just did her job, honestly, quietly. This place was no longer her life. Just a temporary harbor.

What If Staying Isn't Enough?

The newly renovated restaurant was quiet. Mr. Schneider had grand ideas and a dream of transforming a simple beer and sausage place into something more luxurious. He chased investors, changed the design, dismissed Jana's advice and underestimated both the place and its people.

The chef Max was back and the food smelled good, customers came in, the books balanced. Jana was working shifts, earning money, the kids were healthy.

Everything was... functional enough. But something had changed. In the evenings, after she turned off the lights and locked the door, the same question stayed with her: Now what? Not in panic. This time, calmly, practically.

She had survived the worst. Now it was about something else, direction. She wanted to stay in Florida. For the kids. For the weather. For that strange, persistent feeling that, despite everything, she belonged there. But she and the kids' visas were about to expire. Which meant decisions had to be made. They were in a legal grey zone, without any guarantees. And lawyers weren't cheap.

The house they were living in, spacious, a little worn, but theirs, was their only real asset. And the reality was relentless: it had to be sold. Jana was still paying off hospital debts, plus monthly HOA fees.

One evening, after the kids had gone to bed, she sat on the terrace with an open notebook in front of her. She started writing: – Stay in Florida. – Legally. Illegally? – Study digital marketing? – Or apply for a new business, visa and rent a house? – A job that doesn't drain me. That excites me.

– Kids. Stability. Calmness. Writing soothed her. On paper, things looked clearer. There, she could still feel in

control, even if, in reality, she had lost that a long time ago. The house was the last thing they had left. After the divorce. After all the desperate attempts to "start over." But the bills didn't care. The HOA fees came every month. The debts. And worst of all, the hospital bill that had become a nightmare.

She had no health insurance. She couldn't afford it. At first, she hoped it wouldn't

be that bad. But it was. Almost $18,000 for one visit. That's when she knew: she would have to let go of even the last thing—the house. The house would go on the market, whether it hurt or not. Because she had finally learned that nothing in life is saved by clinging to it with all your might.

It wasn't a romantic plan, but one born of hope.

Back Home

Soon after the restaurant sale, the reality hit. The crowd Mr. Schneider expected wasn't there.

Chef Max started drinking more again and Mr. Schneider was left standing alone with his vision.

But one thing he did right. He helped Jana when it mattered most.

Meanwhile, Jana and Carl signed the papers in silence. They arrived at the divorce hearing

separately. Jana in a grey second-hand dress, hair pulled back tight, with a face that no longer expected anything but peace.

Carl in a white linen blazer, and looking like a man

whose mind was somewhere else entirely. Everything had already been divided. and agreed.

She let herself be convinced that a bird in the hand was better than two in the bush.

They agreed to sell below market value. But sometimes, courage means letting go — emotionally too drained to keep fighting.

Jana felt like she had lost in America. She lost the investment. Her family. Her business. But what hurt most was the time she'd lost. Time she could have spent with her kids instead of constantly monitoring Carl.

They split the remaining money 50/50. She took exactly her half. Everything that didn't fit into a suitcase, she had shipped to storage. She didn't ask for anything extra, not even for the children. Still, deep down, she knew Carl would never send them another cent, despite the agreement they both signed.

And then the day came. The flight back to Prague.

The kids slept on the plane, heads resting on her shoulders. Jana stared out the window, watching the lights of Florida fade into darkness, along with everything she had survived over the past five years. There was no euphoria. No grief. Just a quiet inner voice whispering: You made it. Now you're going back. But not as someone who lost.

Her mother was waiting at the airport in Prague. She looked a little older, her face more tired than before,

but her eyes sparkled with joy, and her arms were wide open. The skinny, sun-tanned kids ran to her

and wrapped themselves around her like they were trying to make up for all the months without hugs or stories.

She laughed, tears streaming down her face, repeating again: "Your home. You're home."

Epilogue

If you've made it this far, there's one thing I want to say first: thank you. Thank you

for the courage to stay. Thank you for not closing the book when it started to hurt.

Because I know, sometimes, denying the pain feels easier than holding it. But you stayed.

This book wasn't written to judge. It was written to open a space for courage and

strength, to stand up, and to help others understand what domestic violence really is.

We don't need to go back or stay in the dark, we go back to finally leave it. With open eyes. With a ready heart. And with hands that no longer beg, but create.

Maybe along the way, you found fragments of your own story. Maybe something inside you stirred, something you've long refused to see. And maybe now you're sitting in silence, unsure of what comes next.

That's okay.

Uncertainty is still a step. Silence can be a beginning.

Because the journey back to yourself isn't about perfection. It's about truth. About slow, deliberate steps. About new choices, no longer made out of fear, but out of self-

respect.

This book may be over, but your path isn't.

And if it still feels like too much, know this: no one has to do it alone. And you don't either.

Asking for help doesn't mean you're weak. It means you finally understand, you deserve more.

And you are not alone.

With respect and hope,

Lux Lucens